Handbag

SR

Jillian Powell

Illustrated by Charlotte Alder

Titles in the Full Flight Girl Power series

Download Fever	Jonny Zucker
TV heat	Jonny Zucker
Mer-boy	Justine Smith
Rock Chick	Jillian Powell
Handbag Wars	Jillian Powell
Dark Star	Melanie Joyce
Kelly's Diary	Helen Orme
Striking Out	Jane West
Mystery in Mexico	Jane West
Snowboard Adventure	Alison Milford

Badger Publishing Limited
Oldmedow Road,
Hardwick Industrial Estate,
King's Lynn PE30 4JJ
Telephone: 01438 791037
www.badgerlearning.co.uk

4 6 8 10 9 7 5

Handbag Wars ISBN 978 1 84691 027 2

Series Editor: Jonny Zucker
Publisher: David Jamieson
Commissioning Editor: Carrie Lewis
Editor: Paul Martin
Design: Fiona Grant
Illustration: Charlotte Alder

Handbag Wars

Contents

A New Handbag **4**
An Old Handbag **7**
A Time and a Place **10**
A Dead Cert **14**
A Surprise **18**
The Scent of Success **22**
Good News **26**
A Discovery **28**

A New Handbag

"That is so lush!" Stacey said.

"They had it in blue too," Becks said.

"No. Pink is perfect," Stacey agreed.

Becks held out the bag. "You should get one," she said to Stacey. "They are *so* now."

Stacey and Becks were mad about bags. They had a handbag war going on.

Right now, Becks was winning. She always had the cutest new bag. She had hundreds of them. But it was easy for her. Her mum worked in a shop. She got good deals.

Stacey was losing the war.

"Is that new?" Becks looked down at Stacey's bag.

"No... it's the one I got last year, remember?"

"Oh, yes. I remember. They were everywhere... *last year.*"

Becks turned to go. She flashed a smile at Stacey. Then waved goodbye... with her lush pink bag.

Stacey sighed. Her bag looked *so* yesterday.

An Old Handbag

It was Saturday morning. Stacey was working in the charity shop.

"What shall I do first?" she asked Rita.

"Sort this box of stuff, please, dear," Rita said.

Stacey opened the box. It was mainly clothes. Then she saw the handbag.

It was big. It was black. It was beautiful.

"Hey, Rita. Look at this!" She said.

"Oh! It's a Kelly bag!" Rita said.

"A what?"

"They were all the rage about fifty years ago," Rita told her. "They named them after Grace Kelly."

Stacey looked blank.

"You know!" Rita said. "That beautiful actress who became a princess."

"Oh!" Stacey held the Kelly bag on her arm. It smelt of leather.

"It is so lush… I mean lovely…." she told Rita. "Can I buy it?"

Rita nodded. "No need to price it up then."

Stacey put some money in the till. She so wanted to show Becks. Becks could never match this one.

At home, Stacey opened the bag and felt inside. There was something in a silk pocket. It was a lipstick in a gold case. She read the name. It was French: *La Vie en Rose*.

A Time and a Place

Stacey sent Becks a text.

Fab nu bag. U hav 2 c.

Becks came on the way to school. "It's so glam!" she agreed.

"It's red silk inside," Stacey showed her.

"That's funny!" There was a note inside. Stacey hadn't seen it before. She read it. "Tuesday 4th. 5pm. Banks Hall."

"Today *is* Tuesday 4th. Spooky or what?" Becks said.

"Don't be silly. It's an old note," Stacey said.

Still, Banks Hall was on the way home from school. Stacey got off the bus at the hall. There was a crowd waiting outside. She took out the note again, then a man pushed her inside the hall.

"Right, first on the left!" A woman said to her.

Stacey went where she was told. There were three people sitting at a long table.

"Okay. In your own time," the man said. He nodded to her. "Show us what you can do. Sing. Dance. Whatever!"

Stacey couldn't sing, but she could dance. She did some of her street dancing.

"Thank you! Do you do any tap?" One of the women asked.

"I..."

"Write your details here. We'll be in touch!" the woman said.

A Dead Cert

The next day, Stacey went to see Grandad. She told him about her dancing. Grandad knew she wanted to be a dancer, like her Nan. He was behind her all the way.

"You must have tap lessons," Grandad said.

"Mum says they cost too much," Stacey said.

"Maybe I can help?" Grandad told her.

"No way, Grandad!" She knew Grandad wasn't rich.

"Well, how about we go to the races today?" Grandad said. "Maybe we will get lucky!"

Grandad loved horse racing. He needed cheering up since Nan died. Stacey agreed to go.

When they got there, Grandad took out ten pounds. They looked down the list of horses.

Then she saw it: *La Vie en Rose.* That was it! They had to put the money on that one.

"The odds are terrible!" Grandad said.

The race began. The crowd began to yell and cheer.

"Where's our horse?" Stacey asked Grandad.

"Stacey... Stacey." Grandad was jumping up and down. "It's winning... it's winning... we've come in first!"

It was a big win too.

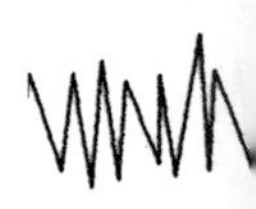

"There's enough here for some tap lessons!" Stacey told Grandad. "Thank you, *La Vie en Rose*!"

A Surprise

The next day, a letter came.

“Mum! I’ve got a part in a new stage show! I’m going to be a dancer!” Stacey danced around. “I have to learn tap… and we start rehearsing in six weeks. I must text Becks.”

Stacey went to get her Kelly bag. She looked inside for her phone. That was funny. There was a green ticket inside. It wasn’t there before. “Mum, did you put this in my bag?”

Mum shook her head. “It looks like a ticket for dry cleaning,” Mum said. “Someone forgot it, I expect.”

Stacey sent Becks a text.

Her phone beeped back on the way to school. Becks sounded as green as the ticket!

After school, Stacey went into town. The ticket had a shop name on it. She found the shop and went inside.

The woman in the shop took the ticket. She looked at the number and went into the back of the shop. Then she came out with a box. "They're all paid for," she told Stacey.

Stacey stepped outside. She opened the box and gasped. It was a pair of tap shoes… *in her size.*

Stacey shivered. This was starting to get weird.

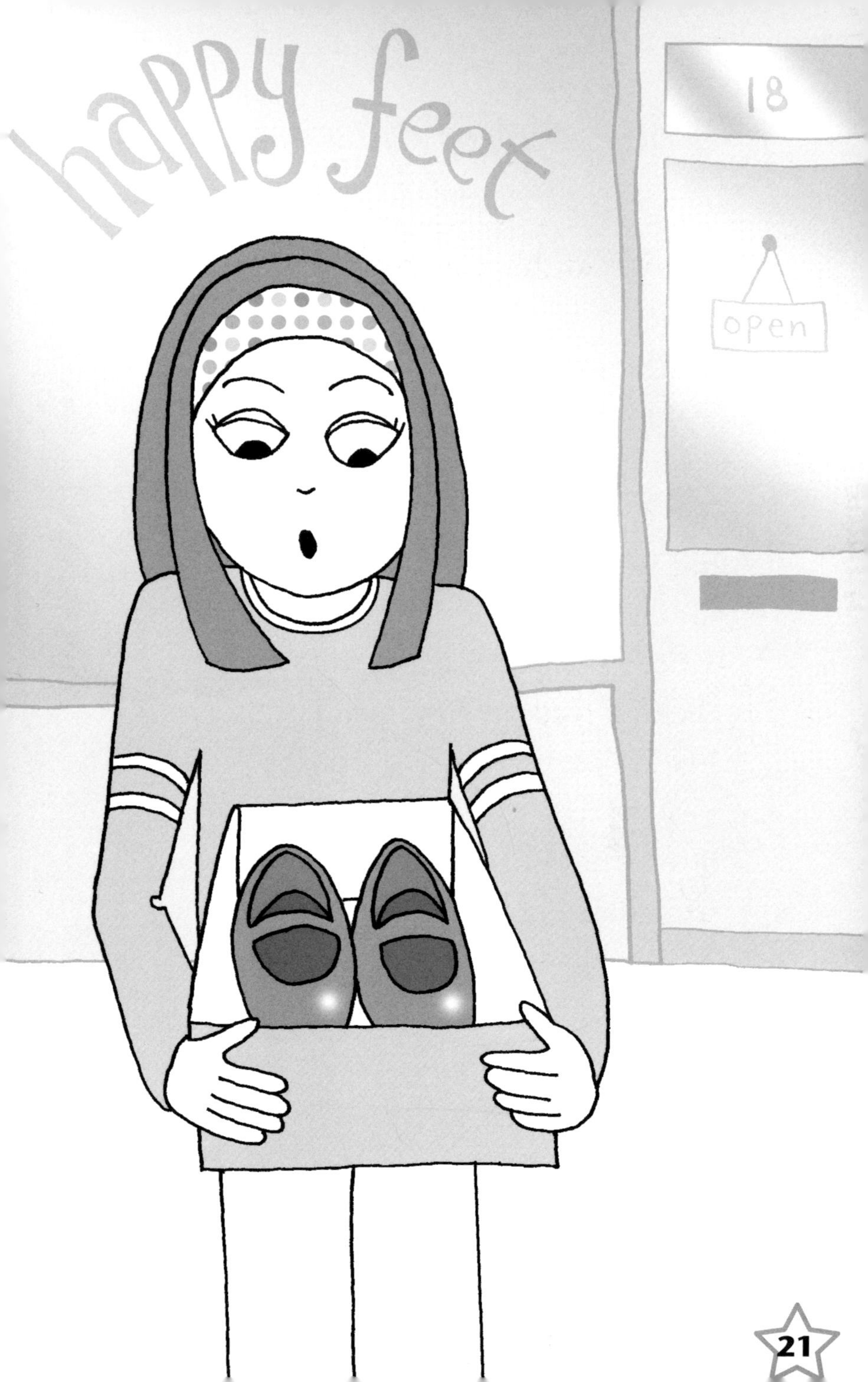
happy feet
18
open

The Scent of Success

The weeks flew by. Stacey loved tap dance. She loved the show even more. She had made new friends too. She still took her Kelly bag out when she went shopping with Becks. Becks had a new bag every time. Stacey didn't envy her any more. Becks was always asking about the show.

Soon, it was the first night. The cast held a party. Stacey dressed up and took her Kelly bag. She was showing it to one of her friends when she found something inside. It was a bottle of perfume.

She showed Mum when she got home.

"It looks quite old," Mum said. "Ask Grandad if he knows what it is."

Stacey took it over later.

Grandad looked at the bottle. He closed his eyes and sniffed. Then he smiled. “New York!” He said at once. “It’s called New York. Your nan used to wear that. She loved it… put too much on sometimes!”

That night, Stacey put the perfume beside her bed. The moon shone on its silver top. Stacey went to sleep thinking about the bright lights of New York.

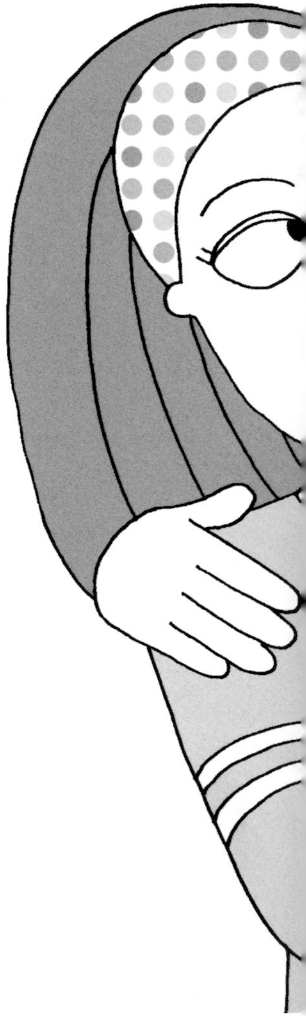

Good News

The show had run for twelve weeks. It was hard work but Stacey loved it. They had great reviews. The cast had their picture in the newspaper. Grandad had been to see it six times. "Your Nan would be so proud!" he told Stacey.

He was there when Stacey heard the news.

It was just after the Saturday night show. The director called the cast together.

"Guys! I have some news for you!" he told them. "You need to pack your bags. We are going to do a run in… New York!"

Everyone in the cast cheered and clapped. But Stacey was quiet. She looked across at Grandad. He winked and smiled at her. Stacey knew he was thinking of the perfume too.

A Discovery

Becks came over the next day. She had told everyone that her best mate was in a show in New York.

"I've got something for you!" She told Stacey. "It's for good luck." Stacey opened it. It was a cute red bag.

"It's *so* now." Becks told her. "You will need it for New York. The girls there are *so* cool. You can't really take that one. I mean, no offence, Stace."

Stacey looked down at her Kelly bag. "Thanks," she told Becks. "I'll text you when I get there, and tell you what the hotel is like."

Later, Grandad came over to see Stacey off. "All packed?" he said.

Stacey nodded.

"You will ring me, won't you? Got your phone?"

Stacey nodded again and held up her bag. Grandad was suddenly silent. He was staring at the handbag.

"Grandad?"

"It's that bag of yours," Grandad said slowly. "It's just like one your Nan had, years ago."

Stacey felt a shiver.

"What happened to Nan's?" she asked Grandad.

"Well, it went to the charity shop with all her other things," Grandad said.

Stacey cuddled the bag. She had to take it with her to New York. It was like having Nan with her all the way. And, after all, she never knew where it would take her next....